MY MOTH

*An Unusual Journey to Becoming a Mother
Through Alzheimer's*

Pam Singleton

Copyright ©2022 *Pam Singleton*

All Rights Reserved.

Table of Contents

Dedication iv

About The Author v

Preface vi

Chapter 1: How Did We Get Here? The Beginning of a Long Road 1

Chapter 2: Understanding the Disease through a Daughter's Eye 13

Chapter 3: Transitioning From Daughter to Caretaker 23

Chapter 4: Applying What My Mother Taught Me Growing Up 29

Chapter 5: The Child I Never Had I Found In My Mother 35

Chapter 6: Learning How to Communicate In a Different Way with Your Loved One 43

Chapter 7: Medication and Other Help 49

Chapter 8: Grieving the Loss of Your Loved One Over Time Before They Die .. 57

Chapter 9: Planning For the Future and Knowing When to Let Go 63

Chapter 10: The Night She Slipped Away 69

Afterward 76

In Closing 78

Dedication

This book is dedicated to my mom, who left us too soon, and my family and friends who supported me when my mom/child was suffering from Alzheimer's.

About The Author

Pam Singleton, MA in Communications, is an adjunct professor at Governor's State University, currently residing in the Chicagoland area.

She teaches Communicating with Someone with Alzheimer's and Leadership classes. She actively participates in the Alzheimer's community and academia.

Preface

I never had children for a variety of reasons. However, I have since come to realize that I did not need to have children as I took care of my mother, who suffered from Alzheimer's disease (AD).

How does that correlate to motherhood, one might ask? Well, simply put, I felt like as my mother went through the seven stages of AD, it felt like I had adopted a 15-year-old teenager and taken care of her until she went through infancy and eventually passed. I got to experience all the ages of childhood but in reverse. I feel that I got the best of both worlds as I got to have my mother for most of my adult life and be a mom to her for nearly 15 years.

I am not the first to share what an awful disease AD is – many books and movies have been made about this topic. But as someone who *lived* it, I feel I bring a totally different perspective to the caretaker and motherhood journey.

I have been trying to write this book for the better part of 10 years, a true labor of love. Although my mother passed in 2011, it has taken years to take shape. Before my mom passed, I was getting my Master's degree in Communications, and I decided to write my thesis on AD. I was years into caring for my mom and felt that I had a great deal of insight, and doing research for the thesis sealed my passion. In addition to writing my thesis paper on "How to Communicate with Someone with Alzheimer's," I wrote a class that I now teach at a university.

I hope that this book brings you some ideas on caretaking and viewing motherhood through a different lens.

"It looks like you are putting on some weight, hun."

When someone has Alzheimer's, they lose their filter.

Chapter 1:
How Did We Get Here?
The Beginning of a Long Road

I will never forget the first time I thought something was wrong with my mom. I had moved back to Illinois from Arizona, and I couldn't believe that the family hadn't noticed what was going on with her. I had been gone for 10 years, and despite being home for all major holidays to see my mom during those years, nobody told me what was happening.

I refer to this family phenomenon as the "white elephant in the room" syndrome. I think all of my siblings and my father knew deep down that something was wrong with mom, but nobody would tell anyone else. We would just cover for her if she had a bathroom accident in an effort not to embarrass her. It was indeed embarrassing for her on some level as she was having bathroom accidents on our couches, in our cars, and while out at the store. We all figured that her timing was off, or she just wasn't feeling well. Little did we know that it was something much more serious.

The confusing aspect to us initially was that my mom had always had bowel issues due to a bout with colon cancer, and so when she started to have accidents, I think we all thought it could have been the case.

My mom was 63 years old when she was diagnosed with Alzheimer's, which was in 1996 – but the truth of the matter is that she had been showing dementia signs for years before that diagnosis.

Once we realized that the whole family was experiencing mom's behavior, we started to share our thoughts about how best to handle the situation. However, this was back in the mid-1990s, and aside from knowing that former president Ronald Reagan had the disease, there wasn't a lot of information available to the public.

To that end, and based on mom's erratic behavior, we often wondered if she was "playing us" off of each other in that, she might be faking her behavior. As an example, some of her behavior was pretty far out there with wild lies about the neighbor having brain cancer and squirrels eating people. We struggled to find the truth in her tales, but it is known that AD can cause paranoia and anxiety. It took us a while, but we finally came to the conclusion that it wasn't a game. It was, sadly, the real thing, AD…..that was stealing our mother away, starting with her mind.

After this point, I think I accepted, at least on an intellectual level, that my mom had AD, but I was not prepared for the emotional toll it would take on all of us, including my mom.

Here are the stages of the disease, and each one is worse than the previous one to the point where the loved one just goes silent.

- *Stage 1: No impairment*
- *Stage 2: Very mild decline*
- *Stage 3: Mild decline*
- *Stage 4: Moderate decline (mild or early stage)*
- *Stage 5: Moderately severe decline (moderate or mid-stage)*
- *Stage 6: Severe decline (moderately severe or mid-stage)*
- *Stage 7: Very severe decline (severe or late stage)*

Stage 1: No impairment:

The person does not experience any memory problems. An interview with a medical professional does not show any evidence of symptoms.

Stage 2: Very mild decline:

Very mild cognitive decline (may be normal age-related changes or earliest signs of AD disease).

The person may feel as if he or she is having memory lapses — forgetting familiar words or the location of everyday objects.

But no symptoms can be detected during a medical examination or by friends, family, or co-workers.

Stage 3: Mild decline:

Mild cognitive decline. Early-stage AD can be diagnosed in some, but not all, individuals with these symptoms.

Friends, family, or co-workers begin to notice difficulties. During a detailed medical interview, doctors may be able to detect problems in memory or concentration. Common stage 3 difficulties include:

- Noticeable problems are coming up with the right word or name.
- Trouble remembering names when introduced to new people.
- Having noticeably greater difficulty performing tasks in social or work settings.
- Forgetting material that one has just read.
- Losing or misplacing a valuable object.
- Increasing trouble with planning or organizing.

Stage 4: Moderate decline (mild or early stage):

At this point, a careful medical interview should be able to detect clear-cut problems in several areas:

- Forgetfulness of recent events.

- Impaired ability to perform challenging mental arithmetic — for example, counting backward from 100 by 7s.

- Greater difficulty performing complex tasks, such as planning dinner for guests, paying bills, or managing finances.

- Forgetfulness about one's own personal history.

- Becoming moody or withdrawn, especially in socially or mentally challenging situations.

Stage 5: Moderately severe decline (moderate or mid-stage):

Gaps in memory and thinking are noticeable, and individuals begin to need help with day-to-day activities. At this stage, those with AD may:

- Be unable to recall their own address or telephone number or the high school or college from which they graduated.

- Become confused about where they are or what day it is.

- Have trouble with less challenging mental arithmetic, such as counting backward from 40 by subtracting 4s or from 20 by 2s.

- Need help choosing proper clothing for the season or the occasion?

- Still, remember significant details about themselves and their family.

- Still require no assistance with eating or using the toilet.

Stage 6: Severe decline (moderately severe or mid-stage):

Memory continues to worsen, personality changes may take place, and individuals need extensive help with daily activities. At this stage, individuals may:

- Lose awareness of recent experiences as well as of their surroundings.

- Remember their own name but have difficulty with their personal history.

- Distinguish familiar and unfamiliar faces but have trouble remembering the name of a spouse or caregiver.

- Need help dressing properly and may, without supervision, make mistakes such as putting pajamas over daytime clothes or shoes on the wrong feet.

- Experience major changes in sleep patterns — sleeping during the day and becoming restless at night.

Stage 7: Very severe decline (severe or late stage):

In the final stage of this disease, individuals lose the ability to respond to their environment, carry on a conversation, and, eventually, control movement. They may still say words or phrases.

At this stage, individuals need help with much of their daily personal care, including eating or using the toilet. They may also lose the ability to smile, sit without support, and hold their heads up. Reflexes become abnormal. Muscles grow rigid. Swallowing impaired.

These stages can last a few months each or a few years, there is no rhyme or reason to the duration, and the disease itself is dreadful. It doesn't care what gender you are, what race, or what social or economic value you are – it does not discriminate.

When we finally took mom to the doctor, we realized that she was well into the 7 Stages of AD (she was in stages 5-6). The fascinating thing about researching this disease is that there was no specific doctor for AD. A General Practitioner (GP) can't diagnose, and there isn't a gerontology doctor of sorts, so the doctor that sees someone with AD is a neurologist, as it is a brain disease at its core.

There is a great book that I read while getting my Master's degree, it is called The 36-Hour Day, and it couldn't have captured the length of a day with someone with AD any better. It is a very long day for all involved. For anyone who is a caregiver to someone with AD illness.

AD is, at its core, a memory disease, and a burdensome part of the journey was realizing that when something occurred in their past, like a death, your loved one might have to relive this over and over every time you tell them.

Another example of the difficulty of the disease is when we took my mom to see her mother's grave. She had begun to lose weight towards the end, so when we got her dressed and into a wheelchair at the cemetery, it was almost as if our mom looked like a mafia matriarch. She was dressed in clothes that dwarfed her, had a blanket over her frail lap, and was wearing big dark sunglasses. My sister and sister-in-law joked about it, and mom didn't think it was funny, but you had to appreciate the comedy of the moment. When she finally got to her mom's grave, she cried as if she had never been there several times prior.

A good guide for us was information that was on the ALZ.ORG website. Below are some symptoms that we knew to watch out for as my mom progressed through the disease.

Ten Warning Signs of Alzheimer's (According to the Alzheimer's Association):

1. Memory loss
2. Difficulty performing familiar tasks
3. Problems with language
4. Disorientation to time and place
5. Poor or decreased judgment
6. Problems with abstract thinking
7. Misplacing things
8. Changes in mood or behavior
9. Changes in personality
10. Loss of initiative

We were fortunate enough during the disease that my mom didn't totally forget any of us. Since my father and I cared for her the most, she would refer to us by different names. My dad was 'that man,' and I was 'hey lady or mom' when she referred to me. I would answer anything she called me as it was easier on her.

There was a long phase during the journey with mom where she would repeat herself (very common in AD patients) not just once or twice but hundreds of times a day. It was often about my dad or our caretakers, and it would be "Where is dad," and I would say, "He is at work," she would say, "Oh," and then repeat that question all day until he came home. It was wearing us down. There were times that I would be sitting with her all day, and I wished I had one of those Office Depot big buttons that I could push to repeat the same answer I had been giving for hours.

Repetition continues into areas of communication that one might not expect, for example, AD patients can usually remember things from the way distant past but not the immediate past. As an example, my mom had a good friend, Betty. One day she asked, "Where has Betty been?" And we had to tell her that Betty had died. She immediately burst into tears screaming, "Betty is dead?" and all we could do was comfort her.... over and over, as this happened every time, she asked about someone who died because she couldn't remember that the people had passed.

Other times, I would be so tired after sitting that I just wanted 5 minutes for a cat nap, and she would be tapping me on the leg saying, "Hun, don't go to sleep, I need you," and my heart would become a puddle of love, and I would sit up and answer her.

And so began our journey with AD.

"Mommy, who is your favorite?"

A comedic question from sisters.

Chapter 2:
Understanding the Disease through a Daughter's Eye

We were lucky enough to take care of my mother at home. I say that because she thrived better when she was with us than she would have in a nursing home, patients are living longer at home than that of life in the facility due to the constant engagement at home.

While teaching my AD class, I have found that many people do not have the luxury or support to keep their loved ones at home. We were blessed to have family members that could pitch in.

In addition to having my father as my mom's primary caregiver, we hired a few women over the years to care for her during the day. Many of the caregivers thought mom was too difficult of a case and quit, but a few hung in there with our family.

I felt very critical of my mom's caregivers as it did feel like I was getting a babysitter for my child, and I wanted only the best for my girl.

One of our caregivers was named Yolanda, but my mom insisted her name was Orlando, so that is what we called her. One strategy we learned about AD over the years was to make their reality your reality, so if mom wanted her name to be Orlando, that's what we did.

My mom liked Orlando so much that one Christmas, mom insisted I take her to the store to get Orlando a gift. Mind you, my mom wasn't very mobile (by choice), as she spent most of her time sitting on her favorite couch. But being taken aback by that request by my mom (now my child), I just wanted to achieve this tiny goal for her.

We bundled up and got in the car. We drove to the store, and we got out, holding hands, and I guided her into the store. Immediately she panicked and said, "I want to go home." I said, "Mom, we just got here," and she started to cry and begged me to take her home. I hugged my mom/child for a long moment realizing that this was when she started to go from the teenager in my care to a frightened child. I told her that I would be right back then we could go home. I quickly ran to get some perfume for Orlando, and we ventured back home, holding hands tightly to get her to her safe place.

Another caretaker that we had through the years was my Aunt Wilma, a lovely strong woman of faith. Wilma is my dad's sister, and we would do things with each other's families for years. But my mom didn't like Wilma as a caretaker, and I think it was because she *knew* my mom, and somehow that made my mom feel humiliated that Wilma was taking care of her. She would scream at her and call her swear words. This was such a departure from my mom's demeanor when she was well, and she was a fairly demure quiet woman of the 1950s. Wilma hung in there and helped my mother for years. It was fleeting, but occasionally my mom would hug her, and I cherished these small victories.

My sister-in-law, Laura, helped with my mom early on, and my mom was fairly open to her assistance, but that wasn't an easy road for my sister-in-law as her mom could be very stubborn with people. But everyone knew this wasn't really Mare, as we affectingly called her, it was the disease.

All of my siblings helped with the caregiving, but I participated in the care often as I was most comfortable with her and her illness. I have three brothers; Rick, Tom, and Gary. I have learned through my own experience and that of my class that some men struggle with taking care of their mothers (with bathroom activities especially), and so my sister Sue and I were the secondary caretakers.

There is a myriad of emotions that one goes through in being a caretaker to someone with AD, and I feel that having your loved one at home raises the bar on these emotions since there is no real break. The feelings run the gamut from love to despair, to hopelessness, to joy, anger, denial, and humor.....sometimes all in the same day.

I touched on making her reality our reality, and this is a coping mechanism that makes it easier for all involved. There would be times that mom would say the sky was black when it was daylight or there were little green men outside her window (paranoia is a common issue with AD). As much as it pained me to agree with her, I would say, "Mom, you are right, there are green men outside. How many are there???" and she would say, "Many, Hun, many."

Let's talk about humor, and one must be careful with this because people with AD have a heightened sensitivity. For example, my sister and I have always joked with my mom about who was the favorite (of course, it was me!), and we would ask her this question during her bad episodes with the disease to try and lighten the moment. However, one time we asked her, "Mommy, who is your favorite" and she started to cry and told us not to make her pick between us. I was so taken aback that I didn't know what to do, so we said we were sorry, but like a small child whose feelings were hurt, she simply sat down and didn't talk to us.

Other times, she loved humor and singing. She loved to sing and slap her leg as she was singing. Her favorite song was Take me out to the Ball Game, and she would sing it all the time. She surprised us by knowing all the words, so we would just sing along. We would break out in song in the car while sitting on the couch or while on the way to the cabin.

Another treat I shared with mom was when we went to the cabin, we would hold hands and lift our hands to the sky as we passed over the Illinois state line into Wisconsin and say "Weeeeeeeeee," and she would cackle, and I would get the biggest kick out of her. To this day, I still perform this little ritual whenever I go to Wisconsin, whether I am alone or with people, and it brings a smile to my face.

I have a very funny story to tell about my mom, and it was at my expense, which is fine. I got a call one evening from one of the caretakers telling me that my mom wanted to talk to me, which astounded me as she had stopped talking on the phone some years ago…..this began because when I would call, she would talk to me for a second then lay me/the phone on the couch and nobody knew she was done with the call, so it surprised me that she called. It turned out that she wanted my address so she could send me a letter. A letter, I thought? How was that even possible since she hadn't written in years?

A few days later, I got a letter in the mail written in my mom's beautiful Palmer-style penmanship, which I have long admired for years (I have my dad's handwriting skills….barely legible). I was so filled with joy over this letter that it brought a tear to my eye before I even opened it. I felt like it was a glimpse into my former mother, what a treat. I started to read it and realized it was written on the back of a *Thank-you* card from my niece's wedding to my parents, but I didn't care. It was *HER* writing in *HER* voice, and I cherished it.

Where is the funny part, you might be asking? Well, some years later, after my mom passed, all my siblings and I were sitting out in the backyard reminiscing about my mom. I became a little overconfident in my prose, piped up that mom sent me a letter a few years back, and I beamed with pride as I said it. To my mild astonishment, they all told me that they also had received a letter from mom. We all laughed very hard, and I have never lived that story down. I still have this letter framed with a picture of my mom on my nightstand.

When a family member has AD, they are out of sorts, and this is incredibly debilitating for them. The truly sad part is that they 'know what they don't know' in some cases. What I mean by that is that they are minutely aware at times that they are sick, but they just can't quite figure out why. As a family, we tried to enrich her life by creating moments for success and eliminating the possibility of failure. We praised her often and, whenever possible, found a way to incorporate humor, it really is the best medicine.

There was an eye-opening symptom that we discovered about AD, and that was that she didn't want to be touched by us or any doctors. It would make her cry out loud in fear, and fear can be very persistent. This issue became a real problem when we noticed that her finger and toenails were growing to the point of curling and digging into her own skin. On her fingers, the problem became so bad that her small diamond ring was cutting off her blood circulation. We emphasized that both needed to be taken care of, but when you are dealing with the mental aspect of AD, there is no rationalizing. Then one day, out of the blue, she let us cut off the ring, thankfully. She cried when this happened, not because of the pain but because we broke the ring.

I did get that ring repaired, shinned up nice, and presented it to her in a beautiful box for Christmas one year, and she loved it so much she cried. She wanted to wear the ring every day, but she was prone to misplacing items, so she could only wear it when I was around. I can still hear her say, "Hun, can I wear my ring today?" And I said, "Sure." We eventually buried her with it on.

My mom loved animals all of her life, especially dogs. We had an Irish Setter for a long time, and they were great friends. As she got deeper into the disease, she started to have a little mean streak in her as it related to pets. For whatever reason, she grew to hate the cat so much that she would toss it across the room or kick it. This mortified me (as I LOVE cats). I tried to reason with her (breaking one of my own coping rules) as I didn't know how to get her to stop. Over time, she just ignored the cat, and the cat lived many long years after that time.

We have a very large extended family, and as far back as I can remember, my mom loved having the kids over for all the holidays. We had Christmas parties, wildly amusing Halloween costume parties, and Thanksgiving, all planned and hosted by my mom. So when she started to cry at these events when she got AD, I couldn't for the life of me understand why something as simple as a happy family gathering would cause such emotions. What I failed to recognize was that her world was getting smaller by the minute. People, as we learned, were too much stimulation for her, and we had to make a concerted effort to rectify this situation. I figured out after reading a few research studies that the stimulation was too much stress for her at one time. To address this, we started having the family members go up to her one at a time and sit with her and hold her hand – this proved to be a very successful tool for us.

I would say the only caveat to that approach was getting the young kids in the family to understand what was wrong with gramma, and I have to say, I am proud of my family for embracing this and allowing their kids to understand that gramma was sick. If she cried or swore, they should not be afraid of her, and they just need to love her anyway, as she can't help that she has AD.

"Take me out to the ball game."

A song from an avid cubs fan.

Chapter 3: Transitioning From Daughter to Caretaker

I never expected to have to care for my parents. We view our parents as strong and larger than life, invincible, and……healthy.

It didn't happen overnight. This caretaker role took more of a sideways trajectory.

My mom was fairly young and healthy when she started to show the signs of the disease. She was in her early 60s, and only 5-10% of the population gets Alzheimer's before they're 65 years old.

In some ways, it was hard for us to decipher the symptoms. My mother suffered from depression her whole life, and some of the symptoms of withdrawing, not sleeping, and speech can elude one, so it took us a little longer to 'accept' what was in front of us…..this AD.

Mom and I were very close growing up as I was the baby of the siblings. I was the 'last' at home, the last to drive, and the last to take care of her well before she got AD.

Mom came from a big family with a lot of siblings, and although she was the baby, she was accustomed to taking care of a few family members, namely her sister, Doris, who suffered from mental illness.

I remember going to Chicago to visit Doris in her transitional housing as she sought treatment for her issues. We would go see her and then go to a Cubs game.

Mom was so patient with Doris, which in retrospect seems pretty amazing since mom suffered from her own demons….. as we would learn later in life.

Mom loved the Cubs, and she was a huge fan, taking pictures with Ron Santo and Billy Williams back in the day. As an avid sports-minded person, I loved this about my mom.

She even came to see me in Arizona, and we would go to spring training games, and when she would see Harry Caray close up, her face would lite up.

Before I started driving, my mom and I would spend many Saturdays together getting her hair done and grocery shopping. Since she didn't drive, my father would drop us off and pick us up.

As the youngest of my family, I got to drive my mom around when I turned 16 and got my driver's license. I didn't care where I was driving to, as I was just thrilled, as a kid, to be driving.

I eventually became the one taking mom to her Saturday appointments, and I thoroughly enjoyed it when we went shopping at garage sales.

I can officially say my mom was 'cool'. In that, she loved all of my friends growing up (some I still have to this day!). She also loved a good holiday party. I fondly remember Halloween, as our family would host this huge dress-up party, and she LOVED dressing up. To this day, Halloween is one of my favorite days, thanks to my mom.

As I started working, I worked weekends at the local mall, and my mom would come to spend a whole Friday night there just so we could eat dinner together during my break. I loved the closeness that we shared.

That closeness didn't falter when I moved to Arizona to transfer with Motorola. I was excited and scared for this next chapter in my life but didn't realize how crushed she would be when I left.

Mom took me leaving very hard, and for years I grappled with guilt over leaving, but I would come home several times a year to see her, and she would even visit.

It wasn't until I had been in Arizona for a number of years that I started to notice a change in her behavior, quieter more withdrawn, and I couldn't pinpoint what it was, but I could feel our roles shifting ever so slightly then.

My mom suffered from depression most of her life, so as a child into a teenager, there was a certain part of me that was taking care of her from an early age. That merely transitioned into a larger role as she showed signs of some illness. We just didn't have a name for it.

I think during this time, I became acutely aware that my mom wasn't like other moms. In fact, she was taking a lot of medications, and she was severely withdrawn. It appeared that her sadness was like a chasm hole that she couldn't get out of….. not even with our help.

A few times while I was in Arizona, things got so bad for mom that she took too many pills and ended up in the emergency room.

While my father couldn't admit the reality of the situation (he thought it was an accident), the rest of us knew the magnitude of the situation, and we sought treatment for her.

She spent the next several years in and out of mental facilities and treatment programs for depression.

During this time, I moved back from Arizona to be closer to my family, especially my mother.

I can distinctly remember sitting on the couch with my mom rubbing her back or patting her head in an effort to take care of her….. in retrospect. I can clearly see now when the shift from daughter to caretaker took place.

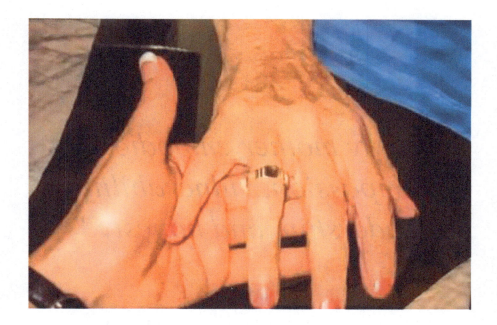

"My mother embodied compassion, vulnerability, leadership, and honesty."

We should all be so lucky.

Chapter 4:
Applying What My Mother Taught Me Growing Up

My mom was always there for me. She attended every school event, parent-teacher meeting, and game.

I didn't know it at the time, but during this time, she was preparing me to be a mom. It just didn't resonate with me. My mother taught me what a true role model is, and for that, I am thankful. As it taught me to be a caring and gentle person, yet stern when I needed to be.

My mother embodied compassion, vulnerability, leadership, and love…… many of the qualities that I not only aspired to but have within me today.

I remember some small things about my mom, too, like she would lay all five kids' clothes out the night before for what we would wear to school the next day….. I still do this to this day with my clothes…. a learned task or a task of love…. you decide.

Was my mother all sugar and spice….. ummm… no! There were many times that I was mischievous growing up that my mother would, on occasion, have to punish me or, God forbid, wash my mouth out with soap.

I feared my mom, the way a child should…. not in a scary way but a respectful one.

When I was 14, the girls' softball team I was playing on had an All-Star team that went to the softball World Series. My mom was active in this journey with us as the mom with the cowbell. She would proudly ring at every game.

One time we went to Kalamazoo, Michigan, for a tournament, and my mom and another girl's mom had missed their high school reunion as they were chaperoning us. I can still remember them in the hallway with a glass of wine, having a great time, laughing, and carrying on. This is one of the few times I saw pure joy on my mom's face. She taught me to let go and enjoy the moment, the ever-precious present. What a great memory for both of us.

All of these things that my mom did for me taught me to be caring and respectful to not only her but all her parents.

As my world shifted to caretaking for her, I could rely on all the elements of my growing up with my mother, which taught me to be a great caregiver.

I have always been a very 'wear my heart on my sleeve' kind of person, but that proved to be very helpful as I cared for my mother because it became my passion.

I was amazed at not only how much stamina it took to be a caretaker but that I had this quiet strength within me to achieve it, but I did.

As a Christian, I leaned heavily on God and my church friends to guide me through this chapter of my life.

I was the first of my friends to have a parent with Alzheimer's, but as time would show, I was not the last. This allowed me to share what I learned with them.

I believe in God's plan for me, and although I have struggled with not being a mother to my own children - I can look back now from my 59-year-old self and see that His plan was to offer me that experience in a unique way to someone that I loved and trusted.

I have said it before and feel it warrants repeating. Caretaking is not for the faint at heart. It is an arduous and long-lasting journey.

As I mentioned, unlike most daughters, I have taken care of my mom on and off for most of my life. My mom instilled in me, without maybe even knowing it, all the skills it would take for me to be a mother to her.

I approached my care with her with, at first, curiosity over the mysterious Alzheimer's disease and then with dignity as we learned how detrimental the disease was.

One must embrace caretaking as if it is the most important thing one will ever do, and for me, it was the most important undertaking I would achieve in my life.

I cared for my mom so deeply and carefully that I know she felt it in my words, actions, and love. Even though she wasn't able to articulate or even reciprocate some of the actions I displayed, I could tell by the look in her deep blue eyes that she knew she was cared for.

I would like to think that she didn't see or feel my frustration at times over the magnitude of the disease or the fact that the disease was stealing her away from me. Being a person of high emotions, I was glad she couldn't read my struggles.

Knowledge IS power, and so I immersed myself in learning my new role as a caretaking mom.

As such, I learned a lot from reading books like [Learning to Speak Alzheimer's](), [A Caregiver's Guide to Alzheimer's Disease: 300 Tips for Making Life Easier](), and the [Alzheimer's Association]().

I would talk to people in nursing homes and hospital advocates when she was in the hospital to get them to understand the disease better. Although there was limited information about the disease, there wasn't a manual for taking care of someone with Alzheimer's.

"Calvin?" "No, Elvis"

"Calvin?" "No, Elvis."

Humor is still possible and necessary with Alzheimer's.

Chapter 5:
The Child I Never Had I Found In My Mother

After months of my mom referring to me as her mom, I didn't really know at the time that it would fill a void for me, but in retrospect, it sure did. My lifelong longing for children was answered by my own mother – I had finally become a mom, albeit a very nontraditional one.

Looking back, all the activities I did with my mom during this time were like spending time with a child. I would take her to all of the family baby and wedding showers, I would shop for clothes with her, and I would take her to our all-season cabin up north.

When I would attend all of these events, the relatives knew that I would be in attendance, and I would no doubt have mom/child in tow, with a diaper bag, wipes, and Depends to be prepared as if I had a toddler. That was what it was like, and I would hold her hand, get her plate for meals, and try and make her feel as normal as possible. But it was a task as even though she was digressing into a childlike state, she was still very much a full-size person with the ability to yell, scream, and stand. My child could be very stubborn, and she would stand up right next to her chair when we went to events. It was like she had a temper tantrum every time we wanted her to sit, and after a while, you learned to pick your battles.

One time, when we went to a baptism for one of my nieces' children, we were in the church, strategically sitting in the back of the church in anticipation of an accident or screaming over, wanting to go home. I could smell that she had gone to the bathroom in her Depends, and like a true mother, I leaned over and peeked in her Depends, and sure enough, it was all over the place. I did this act very respectfully and merely whispered to her that we needed to go to the bathroom, "No," she screamed out loud. Thus began the negotiation to try and get her into the bathroom. But this time, everyone in the church had eyes on us, and eventually, she let me take her to the bathroom, but the mess was too great, and we ended up having to go home. The revelation and this happens a lot, is as much as she wanted to leave places once we got there, she cried when we got home over missing the baptism. It was a constant balancing act to keep emotions in check.

This taking care of our parents with AD gig is not for the weak, and it requires a lot of love, patience, time, negotiation, emotions, and stamina….well, all the things one needs to be a mother, I suppose!

For years my mother loved going to Wisconsin boating (we live in Illinois), and so it was a fairly easy drive of an hour to take her to do something she loved. We did this for years. As the disease progressed, we found it harder to find bathrooms for her to use as we would dock the boat. We would go into restaurants and resorts, but even with a diaper bag and a clean set of clothes, if she needed a shower, we couldn't do that at these places. Our solution was to buy a cabin up there so we would have a place to take her.

One time while at the cabin, she experienced a brief moment of lucidity, a sometimes unheard of but welcomed phenomenon with people with AD. This is where they have a moment of clarity and don't appear to have the disease. While at the cabin, we would usually just hang out and talk or watch TV. I would comb her hair and rub her back.

She was very protective of her fingernails and never wanted them touched. Then one day, she said, "Hun, can you paint my nails?" I was so struck by awe that I ran to the bathroom and got the manicure set and polish. Before she changed her mind, I started painting the nails a beautiful hue of pink, and she just sat there, very present, enjoying this simple pleasure, as if this was something we did every day…. and then minutes later, her AD persona came back. But what a joy to see that flash of clarity…if only for a moment.

We owned the cabin for several years, and she *loved* going to the cabin, to the point where she would ask every time I called or was with her, "When are we going to the cabin," "I want to go to the cabin," and then we would get to the cabin, unpack, and start to get settled in and within minutes she would say she wanted to go home. Like a negotiation with a child, I would try and calm her down and tell her we were going to be staying a little while and that it would be fun.

In order to make her feel conformable at the cabin because she liked her couch spot at home so much, I tried to decorate the cabin in a manner that was very similar to her home, and I know she did feel comfortable there. However, the one thing about people with AD that I learned is that changing their environment is very hard on them since so much of their world is chaos in their head, making her feel comfortable and safe in places we went was my main priority.

Another example of feeling comfortable happened when the family used to come to my house for Thanksgiving. We have a very large family, and it can be overwhelming. But one time, she and my dad slept over, and I was always "on duty" at my house as he was her main caretaker and needed a break.

So she would hang with me during this time, and I would find little things for her to do that make her feel a part of things, as living in the semi-silent world of AD can be very trying on them. I would have her add ingredients to a recipe that was hers, I knew she could no longer make the dish, but she could stir the items or pour the mini marshmallows into the fruit salad, and that made her feel a part of things. This always allowed me the joy of cooking with my child, and we both enjoyed it.

I will say there were many times of joy and happiness but some times of fear too. One time when she came to visit me, she came into my room in the middle of the night and sat at the bottom of my bed. It took me a bit to wake from my slumber to see what she was doing. She was holding a bunch of knives from the kitchen and just said she didn't know what to do with them. It initially frightened me at the thought of her falling down the stairs with knives or, worse yet, hurting herself.

I especially enjoyed walking with her and holding her hand, and this was something we did a great deal. When we shopped or went to the mall or any store or just sat on the couch. I found this very intimate and compassionate that we had this special bond, and I welcomed it with open arms.

I always tell my friends that I learned more about my mom while she was sick than I ever knew when she was healthy. My favorite time to get insights into my mom's life before she got married was while I tucked her in at night. I would get her ready for bed and lay with her until she fell asleep, and she became a chatterbox for a while. She would just spew information.

One night, I remember asking her why she always sings about the harbor lights. As clear as day, she said, "Well, your father was stationed in New York with the Navy before we were married, and I went there one weekend, and he took me to where his ship was docked, and he proposed to me." I had no idea that had happened had we did not have our quiet time, and I would never have known. Shortly after that, I got a speedboat for the cabin, and I named it 'The Harbor Lights' in memory of my mom. I still keep a picture of that boat in my office as it reminds me of her daily. I couldn't have been more proud of my child than I was that night.

As I started to envelop this motherhood role, I have to say some of it was really funny. I would invite my friends over to see me as I was often at my mom's taking care of her, and one friend of mine tried to tell my mother about her little dog, Elvis. My mom screamed back, "Calvin?" "No, Elvis," "Calvin?" "No, Elvis." This went on for a few minutes, and we all laughed, and thereafter the dog became Calvin to my mom.

When I would dream of having a child, I would dream of taking care of them, protecting them, and hugging them all the time. She was only my child for a season in my life but one I will cherish forever. I am grateful that my mom was open to being close and hugging and holding hands. It made me feel so special….at first, it was for HER, but as time grew, it was clearly for ME.

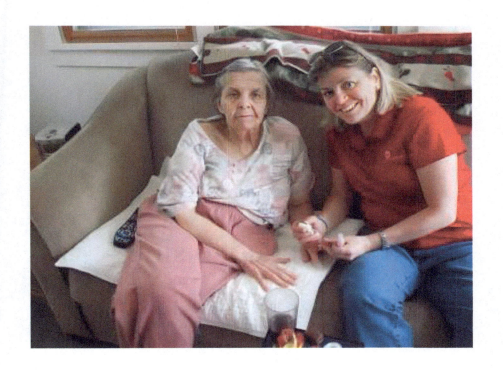

"Sing your little heart out, mom."

Mom loved to sing.

Chapter 6:
Learning How to Communicate In a Different Way with Your Loved One

Studies have shown that communication is comprised of approximately 80% listening and 20% talking. Listening can also take on non-verbal communication, which is what needed to happen with my mom. As she could no longer string her words together to form sentences, thus frustrating her even more into not communicating.

We had to totally alter our method of communicating with her, and this consisted of figuring out ways to still involve her in conversations, parties, and doctors' visits. Since the issue with AD is neurological in nature, the parts of the brain that formulates words started to deteriorate. What I mean is that we needed to find a way for her to engage us without getting her more upset over what she couldn't do, so we focused on what she *could* do. For instance, I found that I could communicate with her in a non-traditional way. What that meant for us was to focus on her hearing and seeing skills more. We ventured into this territory by trying small things, such as, I would label the items she couldn't remember the names of anymore: like the refrigerator, bathroom, and phone, anything that she struggled to recognize.

A few other helpful tips for communicating are: speak clearly to your loved one, use short sentences, make eye contact, give them time to respond, do not interrupt, let them speak for themselves, do not patronize them or ridicule what they say, and communicating through body language. All of these items allow them to still hold on to their dignity, something that is forever slipping away from them.

My mom was not a particularly outgoing person or someone who voiced her opinions, but that all changed with AD, as she would be very vocal about certain topics. We could read her moods based on her facial expressions as she would often stick out her tongue if she didn't agree with you or didn't want to do something, but it did allow us to gauge her reactions. Although this was quite childlike, it was a simple way for us to understand her feelings on the topic. She would do this when we would try to shower her, take her out, and take her to the bathroom.

Crying was another way we knew she was upset, and she would cry about happy events and sad. There were times that I would tell her that someone was sick in the family, and she would react with tears, and other times, I would say that someone was coming over, and she would cry tears of joy. "I haven't seen them in forever," she would say. Although this wasn't the case, she just didn't remember.

We stopped asking her open-ended questions and transitioned to closed-ended questions, such as, "Are you in any pain," "Can you hear me," and "are you hungry." This allowed us a whole new level of communication with my mom.

In addition to how to ask questions, the tone is just as important as the words that are used. My sister, the nurse, worked in critical care departments at the hospital, so her approach to my mom was very clinical and matter-of-fact, whereas mine was a soft, quiet expression. I stress the quiet, not to be talking to her like she is a child but like an adult with a softer tone and delivery. I would sit right next to her and look her in the eyes, too when I talked, so she could feel my love and compassion.

This method of communicating became very useful when we went to the Emergency Room (ER) for various ailments. First off, the ER is never pleasant for anyone, as you are always waiting. For someone with AD, who is out of sorts, filled with anxiety, and not emotionally capable of handling patience, this can seem like an eternity. I would ask the staff to talk to her in short sentences and not full ones. This helped us tremendously.

The most fascinating (and fun) shifting of our communication styles was to allow her more autonomy with her decision-making. While my mom could still dress herself, she would put on sweats and jackets in July and shorts in January, which was not good for our Midwestern weather. I began to offer her outfits to wear, and I knew her favorite color for clothes was purple, so I would pick out three outfits and have her point to which ones she wanted to wear. This allowed her to play a role in her choices and not feel so limited. We employed this same logic with food and watching television.

There are many changes that someone with AD goes through, from changes in their demeanor to their personality and even their palate. I would often cook my mom's food and prepare what she wanted for meals. Since I did this often, I knew her likes, and they were eggs, hamburgers, hotdogs, and of course, Pepsi. What startled me was that when I would cook something for her, like eggs, and I would serve it to her, she would say, in a most adamant voice, "I don't like eggs and never have." Just like that, from one day to the next, her palate changed, and eggs were no longer on the understood menu.

It is like caring for a child at the beginning of their life, where you try to figure out things that they would like or not like to eat based on taste, texture, smell, etc. But in reverse, because you have this baseline knowledge of what she liked her whole life. It's all a trial and error this journey with someone with AD, but you eventually figure out a rhythm that works for your situation.

In an effort to record my mom for posterity, I would try and record with my phone our pillow talks when I put her to bed. It was a great way to learn about my mom while saving it for later, and I have since realized hearing her voice years later still melts my heart. Most of the time, she would let me do it, but occasionally she would say, "Hun, what are you doing over there?" "I am recording us, mom," so I would have to cover it up with the blanket…..but still secretly keep the recording going. Truth be told, I think she liked this little recording game we played.

"I am sorry I am sick."

A rare moment of lucidity with the disease.

Chapter 7:
Medication and Other Help

Medication and marketing have always interested me as it seems that these two are not mutually exclusive, although you wouldn't know that from the marketing of medications. There seem to be many liberties taken with the marketing of medications, especially in the AD arena. There are two main medications for AD: Aricept and Namenda. Both of these are marketed to say this medication *can* treat the disease but not slow the progression or cure the disease. That one word, *can*, changes the whole sentence and gives people false hope for their loved ones. I know it did for us.

One of the well-known facts in the medical industry is that there is no cure for AD, nor is there a treatment (medication or otherwise) to slow the progression. Once you get the disease, it is basically a death sentence. The tragic part about this is that people like my mom can suffer from it for years if they have no other ailments, making it a very long road to a horrible quality of life.

I hope in my lifetime to see a cure for AD, but the truth of the matter is that bringing a drug to market is a very daunting and drawn-out process.

At a conference that I was at in 2019, I learned that there are so many different paths that AD research can take. Determining which one to have the scientist work on is like a crap shoot, in that there are hundreds of issues with the pathways in the brain related to AD that to pick just one to test and develop a drug for can take up to 15 years. The other major issue is the cost of bringing a drug to market, which can take hundreds of millions of dollars.

One might ask why more pharmaceutical companies are not producing AD drugs, and my personal option is that AD treatment is not a money maker as opposed to a drug for blood thinners or cholesterol.

The best we can do, and we have done this many times with mom, is to treat the symptoms, such as anxiety and sleeplessness. We would give our mom valium to calm her down before bed, before company came over, and even before caretakers came to help her.

I found that before I would give my mom a shower (which she HATED taking), I would give her a pill to relax her as she was so humiliated at me giving her a shower after a bathroom accident that she would be mortified and cry.

One time, when she wouldn't get in the shower, I had to strip down and get myself in the shower with her, and with tears streaming down her face, I looked into her beautiful blue eyes and said, "I am so sorry mom," and she would say, "I am sorry I am sick Hun, you know I got the ax-heimers." That was how she pronounced Alzheimer's. It just broke my heart in two to see my mother, as my regressing child, crying and hurting so much. I told her, "Mom, it isn't your fault, you are sick, and you can't help it." I just held her and then washed her hair and body and got her dried off and back to the comfort of her couch with her Pepsi.

Another tool we used from our toolbox was an encouragement of sorts for taking a shower or going to the bathroom. She loved Pepsi, and although we didn't want her drinking pop all day, when I knew it was time to shower or eat or whatever we needed to do with her, I would promise her a Pepsi once she was done. I supposed this could be misconstrued as manipulation. However, to us, it was just a means to an end, and it worked nearly every time. For those of you that struggle with this aspect of the disease, try this persuasive tactic.

The other resources available to you are in your community. They are respite care, adult day care, and visits from social services. These services were instrumental for us in caring for mom. Respite care is available at many nursing homes, and the way it works is that if you need a break (and it is OK to say you do), then you can arrange for your loved one to stay in the facility for a few days. The adult day care is open to anyone, but they do gauge where you are in the 7 Stages of AD so as not to put the other patients in any danger. Lastly, for visits from social services, we would have a Certified Nursing Assistant (CNA) come in two times a week to shower mom and check her vitals. This was also when we would use the valium to ensure that mom wasn't combative.

There is an interesting story about our experience with Adult Day Care. We signed mom up for it when she was still in the mid-stages of AD. We did this so that she could interact with other like-minded people, but after a few days of trying this, the daycare called us and said mom was mean to the other clients, and she couldn't come back. This didn't seem to surprise mom as she didn't want to go anyway. But as the mother figure, I felt like my child was accused of being a bully, and I wanted to try and explain to them that she couldn't help it. She didn't know what she was doing or saying, but instead, so as not to 'bother' other people, we kept mom home and out of the public eye as her illness progressed.

As a person who has the emotional aptitude of a small child, mom's feelings would get hurt very easily, and it was tough to explain to her why people (especially kids) were mean to her or laughed at her. I went to many doctors' appointments with my child, and our primary doctor was a GP, and they had a lot of kids in the waiting room. My mom wouldn't sit down on many occasions, and I would try and reason with her to please sit down, and she would yell and stick her tongue out at me. Of course, this made the kids laugh, but what my child didn't understand was that they were laughing *with* her, not *at* her.

From a caretaker's perspective, there are many studies about how much time caregivers spend taking care of loved ones and even more data on how this impacts the caretakers' health by the impact it has on their own bodies.

- 6.5 million people in the U.S. are living with Alzheimer's
- The direct and indirect costs of this to Medicare, Medicaid, and businesses are $321 billion annually.
- 16.1 million Unpaid caregivers provided an estimated 18.5 billion hours of unpaid care valued at more than $272 billion.
- Every 66 seconds, someone develops Alzheimer's.
- 70% of Caregivers suffer from depression with feelings of Prolonged saddened mood, Insomnia or other sleeping problems, and sudden weight gain or loss.

All caregivers *need* breaks in order to take care of themselves. This was very important for me. As much as I tried to grieve and decompress along the way when I would leave my mom, I would often draw myself a bath and have a glass of wine to try and re-ground myself into a better emotional state.

I tried a tactic during my time with mom of taking breaks whenever I could and imploring others to do the same thing for their health. We went through this with our own father, too, as he was in his late 70's trying to take care of her, and it was too much for him. This was when we hired caretakers.

It is imperative that you have a support system to be with your loved one on the AD journey. I was blessed enough to have a strong church family, many friends, and a family basically going through it with me.

I also did a lot of community outreach on AD. I was like a sponge during this time, taking in as much information as I could and trying to immerse myself in finding out about the disease. I was shocked to find out how much information *wasn't* available in the community. As such, as I was already doing research on AD for my Master's degree, I wanted to put what I was learning into practice.

I reached out to several nursing homes, hospitals, and libraries to see if I could come and present about my AD journey and teach people how to communicate with someone with AD. I was thrilled that a few people reached back out with interest in me coming to the present. To that end, I would present to all shifts of the nursing homes, the memory wing of the hospital, and Lunch & Learns at the library. It was not only a great way to share the information with people but also learn about how other people are coping as caretakers for people with AD.

The people I was training soaked up the information and asked lots of questions. This part of the training was very healing for me to do as it helped me and the others in the room. I have always believed that it takes a special person, almost like a calling, to be able to work with people with AD. I have met some wonderful people along the way who answered this calling.

"It is like losing a small part of your soul one piece at a time."

This journey of Alzheimer's.

Chapter 8:
Grieving the Loss of Your Loved One Over Time Before They Die

Spending time with a loved one with AD is like spending time in a recording studio in that you get to listen to the same tracks over and over. The good part about that is there is communication that can still occur, the bad part is that it gets harder to decipher and understand, and you see all the decline, knowing it will never get better.

They say with people who suffer from a terminal illness, you lose a little bit of that person every day, and this is most certainly true for AD. It is like losing a small part of your soul, one piece at a time.

I started teaching my Alzheimer's class while my mom was still alive, and I would explain to the class that every time I saw my mom, it was like meeting a new person over and over. It weighs on you and can bring you down, but I always felt like I couldn't break down in front of her, and therefore, I wasn't able to grieve. But I felt like I was grieving her every time I saw her as I would lose a part of her personality, behavior, laughter, smiles, etc.

When my mom passed, I didn't cry. This both surprised and disappointed me as I thought that I *should* be crying since I had just lost my mother/child.

As I grieved, I think I wondered if I spent enough time with her, the guilt side of grief. However, I had spent a great deal of time with her through the years, so I wrestled with this thought for a long time until I finally realized that I was given this gift of being able to spend time with her…as my mother and my child.

In a way, I lost two separate people, my mother and my child. Those were two totally different grief processes and occurred over years while she was alive and after she passed. The thought of not being able to ever hold my mom's beautiful hands again was devastating thought, but I couldn't stay in denial about the progression and how I needed to take care of myself in this process too.

I would save my grieving for my drive home on Sundays after weekends with my mom. I lived 90 minutes away from her, and I would spend a great deal of this drive home sobbing over the loss of who my mother was to me.

Grief, no matter when you choose to do it (or when it *chooses* to impact you), is a very difficult emotion at times. This is especially true when you are still caring for the person. It's like being in the middle of a fire without a hose.

I would often talk to my dear friend, Gail, who was experiencing a similar road with her mother. We both struggled to grasp the reality of our awful situations with our moms, and we looked to God for peace, patience, and understanding. We would often talk about how crucial our faith was and for people who didn't have faith, we don't know how they cope.

Even when one is caring for someone with AD, there has to be a part of them that wonders, "Will I get this horrific disease?" and yes, I have wondered. I have kept up my research on this topic for my class but with a keen eye on a cure and any developments for slowing the progression.

A few years back, there was talk of a study at Indiana University about a blood test that you could take to determine if you had a *predisposition* for the disease. It didn't tout that it would reveal if you had AD, just whether or not there was a chance you might get it.

I ask this question to my class every semester, and most students are split 50/50 on whether they would take the test. My feeling is that I won't take the test as I believe in the divine plan, and I try to take life as it comes.

Even before my mom passed, I was buying grieving books. I had not really experienced the death of a loved one as an adult, and being the Type A personality that I am, I wanted to intellectually prepare for this as much as possible. The part that escaped me, though, was that grief is an emotional journey over time, not a checklist to be done in a particular order. Ultimately, grief is messy.

The grief that you experience while your loved one is still alive is ever present. I have always been someone who has had a soft spirit, felt things deeply, and wasn't afraid to let those tough emotions inside…..and then let them go. It is a process that has been effective for me for years. Sometimes the feelings like to stay longer than I would prefer, but they eventually dissipate. This was (and still is) the case with grieving my mom.

"Put me in my panda pajamas so people will like me in heaven."

Mom's favorite outfit.

Chapter 9: Planning For the Future and Knowing When to Let Go

I never dreamt that I would actively be planning my mother's funeral while she was still alive, but I made it my mission to communicate with her as best I could to plan something that would make her happy.

To that end, as we got within the last 6 months of her life (based on her behavior and her weight loss), we knew that she was continuously declining. I decided to broach the topic of death with her. I didn't want her to be afraid, so I was very careful with the words I chose when we talked about it, but she was surprisingly receptive to the topic.

My child and I were able to talk openly about what she wanted at her funeral. I asked her, "Do you want yellow roses?" (they were her favorite), and she said, "yes." We talked about what outfit she wanted to be buried in, and immediately her Panda pajamas came up. "Put me in my Panda pajamas so people will like me in heaven." I let her know right then that God didn't care what she would be wearing – he would welcome her no matter what.

I told her she needed to have a pretty blouse for everyone to see her in but that we could put her pandas in the casket with her.

As we talked about what else she wanted for the funeral, we switched to music. Mom loved Christmas music and Country and Western. But she said for us to pick out the music, so it was left to my dad to pick out the songs. I added worship songs and Took me out to the ball Game.

One wouldn't think that you can let go before someone dies, but with AD, it is needed to be able to be there for your loved one. It isn't letting go in the traditional way but more for the caretaker to be able to emotionally adjust in their head how to view their loved one.

Once we accepted the fact that our journey was to deal with the AD, we needed to let go of *who* mom was; as a person, a mom, a child, all of it. After you let go of this aspect, it makes dealing with the topic a little easier.

I viewed my responsibility for my mom as if I was a party to her Power of Attorney (POA). In that, in an odd way, my father and I 'shared' custody of my mom. We both mutually agreed to have an understanding that if something happened to her and she needed to go to the doctor or hospital, we would talk collectively about her care and any decisions that needed to be made.

This process with my dad wasn't always easy, as we had different approaches to her care. I, having done the research, knew the importance of treating the symptoms mom was experiencing. These symptoms include anxiety, agitation, sleeplessness, and paranoia. I used an anti-anxiety medication to keep her calm and preserve her quality of life as best I could. Whereas my father felt that I was overmedicating her, but I was merely looking for a better way for her to live.

We eventually came to respect each other's perspective on mom's care as we were both coming from a place of love.

As I have mentioned in Chapter three, taking my mom to the ER was a very onerous chore, and there were times when medications to calm her were needed. Another mechanism that I learned was helpful when at the ER was the have the POA, Living Will, and any health directives at the ready when we went to the hospital, and this would help the staff understand our unique situation.

When you are caring for someone with AD, there is always a part in the back of your mind that wonders how soon they will die, it never really leaves your mind. Having this insight actually proved to be very useful to me as I knew letting go was a part of the process of caring for someone with AD.

"Am I going to heaven?"

The importance of spirituality in the journey.

Chapter 10:
The Night She Slipped Away

I have said this many times in my life, but as much as we planned for mom's departure from this world, one is never ready for it when it actually happens.

The night my mom/child started to slip away was a night like any other. We had a steady routine when I spent the night, and for this particular week, my sister and I were tag teaming mom on all shifts as my dad was away on a fishing trip.

I was taking the evenings and overnights and working during the day, and my sister had the day shift.

It was Monday evening, June 13th, 2011, my first overnight of the week, and I treated it like any other. I prepared mom's food, which at this point had to be pureed as she stopped feeding herself and being able to take solid foods, and we watched a DVD version of a Chicago Cubs game from another day. Once the WGN news was over for the night, I went to put mom to bed…..cleaned her, brushed her dentures, and got her pajamas on, panda pajamas, her favorite.

As a mother at this time, it was like putting a toddler to bed. She was eager for me to say and not turn off the lights as she didn't want to fall asleep alone in the dark. I enjoyed this time as well, as I got to talk to her about anything. We talked about heaven, and she shyly asked, "Am I going to Heaven?" "Yes," I exclaimed. She was so excited to hear this answer that she was beaming so much you could almost see the light coming off her face, despite being in the dark.

On this night, we talked about God, as she attended church as a child, and what kind of church activities she remembered. It has always amazed me how people with AD can remember things from 50 years ago but can't remember names or if they ate. We talked about this for a little bit as I was very active in my church's Sunday school program and Christmas plays, and my mom loved hearing all about the kids.

As I turned out the light, she wanted to make sure that I was still lying next to her in her bed, so she reached her hand over to touch me, and I was there. At a certain point, she asked, "Can you see the light in the sky" and I said, "No, mom, I am unsure what you are seeing, but I don't see it." As time went on, I reflected on my own thoughts about our talk about God and being saved and going to heaven, and I wondered if an angel was somehow appearing to her. I told her to reach for the light (it brings tears to my eyes every time I tell this story), and I could see her hands go up towards the ceiling, the sky, and maybe the waiting angel.

I awoke the next morning still in her bed and asked if she was ready to get up, and I didn't get a response. I immediately felt panic in my chest but confirmed that she had a pulse, but she was not awake. I tried to move her legs to the side of the bed as if to get her to stand, but she was like dead weight, and my heart began to race even harder. I didn't know what was happening and so I called my sister, the nurse, and asked her to come over immediately.

I lay with my mom/child until my sister arrived, tears streaming down my face at the thought of not only losing my mom but the child I longed for as well. It was a deep seeded feeling of sadness and fear, and it felt like it at that moment, like I couldn't escape the feelings. My sister arrived and determined that my mom/child had somehow slipped into a coma.

The next few hours were a blur for me as we called our social worker to send someone to the house and prepare for the inevitable. I spent time calling my siblings and their kids to tell them what was going on. Within a matter of hours, we moved my child from her bedroom into a hospital bed, looking out one of the bay windows in the living room. Although my child couldn't speak due to the coma, we tried to give her a beautiful place to look out as she lived out her seemingly final days.

My father, who was in Canada at this time, wasn't grasping the gravity of the situation. Although I can't necessarily blame him, mom has rallied many times in the past from death's bed, and so he chose to stay in Canada for a few more days. I always joke that my dad didn't take the news from me seriously, but he would from my sister, the nurse.

As Monday bled into Tuesday and Wednesday of that week, family members gathered around mom, not knowing at all that I was silently suffering at the thought of losing my mom *and* my child. My sister (the nurse ☺) eventually convinced my dad of the seriousness of the situation, and he said he'd be home late on Thursday.

During these coma day's family just sat with mom, talking to her and hugging her. By this time, she truly did look like an infant, curled into a fetal position with socks on her hands so she wouldn't scratch her face. She just looked like she was sleeping.

We knew what had happened. She slipped into the coma because she failed to thrive, a loose medical term given to people who either medically or emotionally just give up and stop taking food into their bodies and subsequently have no output either. To this point, we had elected years ago to make mom a Do Not Resuscitate (DNR) and not use any heroic measures, including a feeding tube. We knew it would just be a matter of time before she passed.

As my siblings and I gathered around my mom, we would often ask my sister, "How Long?" and as we entered into Thursday night, she said, "Not long. Her breathing is more labored."

My father eventually arrived home late Thursday afternoon and was stunned at the state my mom was in. Although we tried to prepare him during our phone calls, I am sure it was quite a shock to see his wife of some 50 years in this coma state.

After seeing her briefly, he went into his office, still struggling to digest what he saw in my mom's condition. We tried to tell him while he was in Canada that it was dire, but like many scenarios in life, when something smacks you in the face, it hits home deeply.

My sister and I went into the office to talk to my dad and explain to him our thoughts about mom still not quite letting go. We figured she was waiting for him to get home from Canada, but I had not really believed, prior to this, the power of love and the intersection between that and letting go. We expressed to him that he had to actually SAY the words to her. He seemed dumbfounded by this request, and I am sure a part of him didn't want her to go, despite her current state.

Eventually, he went to her bedside and, through tears, said the words loud enough for her to hear and, in a most compassionate tone, said….. "Mary, you can let go……" and within a matter of minutes, she drew her last breath. It still gives me the chills to think about that moment and how she waited for the love of her life to come home so she could let go of the long fight.

The field nurse came not too long after that to pronounce mom, and when asked what time my mom passed, out of the blue, my sometimes very shy brother Tom said pointedly, "5:10."

The rest of that night was a blur as a flurry of people came to the house to honor my mom.

What caught me off guard a little was that my father wanted to plan the funeral right away. She passed on a Friday, and the wake was Monday, and the funeral was on Tuesday. To me, that was too fast to adjust to the reality of the situation. He was the husband, and it was his decision, and we honored his wishes.

We planned a beautiful funeral for my mom, and it was very nontraditional because I put her favorite pajamas, her Pandas, in the casket with a can of Pepsi and a Cubs hat....all things she loved. As my mom's/child's body was being taken out of the funeral home, we played an array of music, which included, of course, Take me out to the ball game.

I am grateful to God for the opportunity and the gifts of compassion and love to carry out my caretaking. I got to live out my lifelong dream of being a mom. Life is defined by the choices we make, and I am thrilled that I choose to take care of my mother …… and my child.

Afterward

The AD journey can be a different experience for each family. No two people are alike. Although they might all suffer similar symptoms of AD - the manner in which your family approaches the disease might take some trial and error to find the right recipe for success. I've brought some communication tips to the table in this book that, hopefully, you can apply in the caretaking of your loved one. Remember…..no baby talking, and always treat them with dignity.

I've also touched on what my mom was like before AD, in that some of her lifelong depression was likely a contributing factor to her AD. What made this particular aspect more palatable for me in her caretaking was that I was keenly aware long before her AD that she was extremely sensitive, and I learned how to cope with this and treat her from a place of love and understanding. This uniquely prepared me for her care. Both as a mother and a child.

The way in which she raised all of her children instilled in us discipline, a good work ethic, and compassion. These traits have served me well, both personally and professionally. I addressed grief, although we might all be familiar with the 5 stages of grief, grieving someone with AD is totally different. My takeaway for you is to grieve a little bit at a time 'before ' they pass. This will allow you to remember how your loved one was before they died….and not how they were with AD.

Motherhood…..the crux of the book for me - I hope you can see the motherhood role in a new light. There are so many ways one can be a mother figure, and it can take on many forms- not just the traditional one. I certainly learned a lot from my glorious experience with my child, and for that, I will be forever thankful.

In Closing

It's been eleven long years since my child passed, and not a day goes by that I don't think about her as my mom or as my child.

Alzheimer's is an awful disease and although I feel terrible that my mom had to endure it for those 15 years, had she not, I wouldn't have been able to experience my own mini version of motherhood.

I am grateful to my church, my friends, and my family.

I also want to thank all the students who have taken my classes and shared with me their heartaches and joyful experiences with the disease, for, without them, I wouldn't have a story to tell every semester, and I will continue to educate people on this disease and to tell my mother, my child story for years to come.

Made in the USA
Monee, IL
24 September 2024

66544433R00049